P9-DJA-657

DOG DIARIES

STUBBY

DOG DIARIES

#1: Ginger

A puppy-mill survivor in search of a *furever* family

#2: Buddy

The first Seeing Eye guide dog

#3: Barry

Legendary rescue dog of the Great Saint Bernard Hospice

#4: Togo

Unsung hero of the 1925 Nome Serum Run

#5: Dash

One of two dogs to travel to the New World
aboard the *Mayflower*

#6: Sweetie

George Washington's "perfect" foxhound

#7: Stubby

One of the greatest dogs in military history

BY KATE KLIMO • ILLUSTRATED BY TIM JESSELL

RANDOM HOUSE, NEW YORK

JOHN C. HART MEMORIAL LIBRARY
1130 MAIN STREET
SHRUB OAK, NEW YORK 10588
PHONE: 914-245-5262

The author and editor would like to thank Catharine Fronk-Giordano, Archivist, Stars and Stripes Library and Archives, Washington, D.C., for her assistance in the preparation of this book.

This is a work of fiction. All incidents and dialogue, and all characters with the exception of some well-known historical and public figures, are products of the author's imagination and are not to be construed as real. Where real-life historical or public figures appear, the situations, incidents, and dialogues concerning those persons are fictional and are not intended to depict actual events or to change the fictional nature of the work. In all other respects, any resemblance to persons living or dead is entirely coincidental.

Text copyright © 2015 by Kate Klimo
Cover art and interior illustrations copyright © 2015 by Tim Jessell
Photographs courtesy of Division of Armed Forces History, National Museum of American History, Smithsonian Institution, p. ix; Harris & Ewing Collection (Library of Congress), p. 150

All rights reserved. Published in the United States by Random House Children's Books, a division of Penguin Random House LLC, New York.

Random House and the colophon are registered trademarks of Penguin Random House LLC.

Visit us on the Web! randomhousekids.com

Educators and librarians, for a variety of teaching tools, visit us at RHTeachersLibrarians.com

Library of Congress Cataloging-in-Publication Data
Klimo, Kate.
Stubby / by Kate Klimo ; illustrated by Tim Jessell. — First edition.
pages cm. — (Dog diaries ; [#7])
Summary: "Stubby the war dog narrates the story of his life, from his birth on the streets of New Haven, Connecticut, through his time spent in Europe with the American Expeditionary Forces, to his eventual hero's welcome back in the U.S."
—Provided by publisher.
Includes bibliographical references.
ISBN 978-0-385-39243-3 (trade) — ISBN 978-0-385-39244-0 (lib. bdg.) —
ISBN 978-0-385-39245-7 (ebook)
1. Dogs—War use—Juvenile fiction. 2. World War, 1914–1918—France—Juvenile fiction. [1. Dogs—War use—Fiction. 2. Working dogs—Fiction. 3. World War, 1914–1918—France—Fiction. 4. France—History—1914–1940—Fiction.]
I. Jessell, Tim, illustrator. II. Jessell, Tim, illustrator. III. Title.
PZ10.3.K686Stu 2015 [Fic]—dc23 2014025497

Printed in the United States of America

10 9 8 7 6 5 4 3 2 1

First Edition

Random House Children's Books supports the First Amendment and celebrates the right to read.

For Paul Klimo, USMC

—K.K.

It's not the size of the dog in the fight;
it's the size of the fight in the dog.

—T.J.

CONTENTS

Conroy (left), Stubby, and another soldier in Beaumont, France, 1918

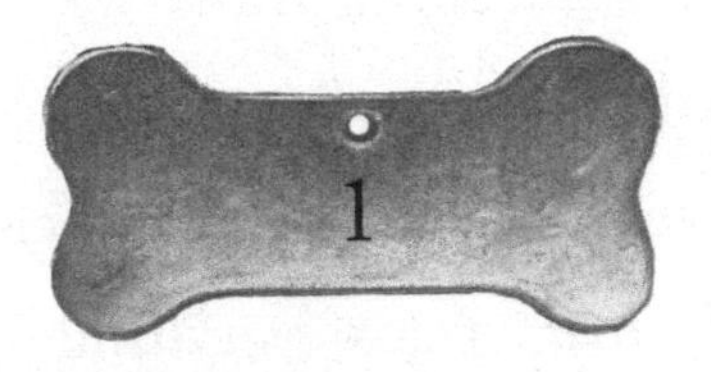

STREET DOG

Make no bones about it: I'm a street dog—born in an alley behind a New Haven diner. A hash slinger with a heart of gold looked the other way while Mom dropped her umpteenth litter in a pile of empty spud sacks. Not too much later, she took off after the butcher's wagon. From then on, it was every pup for himself. I soon lost track of my littermates.

I did all right on my own. I scrounged for

scraps, stood up to dogs bigger than me, and slept wherever I could. The street was my home. But that didn't mean I wanted to spend the rest of my life there. Sure, I was a mutt. Mom was an American Staffordshire bull terrier. Pop was who knew what. From her, I got my solid build and crew-cut coat. From my old man, I got everything else, like my drooping jowls and my bug eyes. With my looks, I wasn't aiming to win any beauty contests. But I was a good dog. If some stand-up person were to give me half a chance, I'd show them just *how* good a dog I could be.

My pals on the street thought I had a screw loose. We used to meet up now and then at the Dumpster behind the deli. We'd shoot the breeze and share tips on the choicest pickings or the meanest shopkeepers. I always asked if they'd seen anyone who looked like they needed a pet.

With a mug like yours, who'd want you? Stinky cracked.

She was one to talk! She smelled so bad, she could clear an alley faster than a dogcatcher.

People like a dog with a nice tail, said Scruffy. She looked like a dust ball with fangs, but Scruffy's tail was a thing of beauty. She never let us forget it. *You've got nothing to wag but a stump.*

True enough. In the tail department, you might say I'd been shortchanged. My tail was not much bigger than the chewed stub of a cigar. That's how I came by my name: Stubby.

There's more to being a good dog than wagging a tail, I said.

True, but why would you want to be owned? Scruffy said. *The street is the only place for a self-respecting dog. The pet's life is for suckers.*

Then call me a sucker, because I was fed up

with eating garbage. I'd had it with being chased by shopkeepers and swatted by little old ladies who thought I was after their groceries. (I probably was, but that didn't mean they had to get nasty about it!) Give me a collar, two squares a day, and forty winks a night with a roof over my head, and I'd sit up and say please, thank you, and the Pledge of Allegiance of these United States. Of course, the chances of this ever happening were slim to none, but a dog could dream, couldn't he?

Then one day, things began to look up. The United States Army came to town! They arrived by the truckload, more young men than you could shake a stick at, all dressed alike in spanking-clean olive-drab shirts and trousers and boots with a spit shine. They came to have a good time. New Haven's restaurants spilled over with them. This was good news for street dogs. More people meant more garbage. But I had bigger fish to fry. I was on the lookout for someone to take me home. I didn't kid myself. I knew I was too ugly to be a lady's dog and too tough-looking to be trusted with a toddler. But a nice, clean-cut young man? Now *that* might be the ticket.

I waited on the curb as one of the army trucks pulled in. Out of the back piled a pack of—you guessed it—clean-cut soldier boys.

Hey, guys, this is your big opportunity! I said, putting on my most adorable puppy-dog face.

Jeez, Louise! These guys walked right past me without a second look. Was I invisible or something? And then another soldier jumped down from the truck. He looked straight at me. "Hey, dog," he said. "Who are you? The welcoming committee?"

You got that right, pal. Welcome to your life as a future pet owner!

He bent down and scratched me behind the ear. *Ooooh.* How did he know that was my sweet spot? Then his two buddies joined him, and off he went down the street.

Naturally, I followed. He and his buddies made their way to an eatery on Main. I didn't go inside, of course. I knew better than that. I staked out the side door on the alley. I knew the owners would shoo me away from the front. But maybe I'd get lucky and he'd come out the side door for a breather. And if he did—*bam*—there I'd be. *Hey, buddy, can I interest you in a charming bull terrier mix? I'm five months old and housebroken.* I've been told that's important to people. They don't like dogs doing their business indoors. Not that I'd ever set paw inside of a house. But if I did, you can bet I wouldn't lift my leg on their precious turf.

The side door swung open. Loud laughter and

music spilled out, along with the smell of meat sizzling on a griddle. I leapt to my feet.

Drat!

It was just a guy in an apron wheeling out a can of trash. He wasn't any happier to see me than I was to see him. He waved his arms and chased me down the alley. Just in case I didn't get the message, he grabbed a handful of gravel and threw it at me.

Yow—that smarted!

Scooting around the corner, I waited until the coast was clear, then crept back to my post.

The next time the door opened, I skittered back away, just in case it was Apron Man. But this time, it was my soldier boy! He leaned up against the side of the building, closed his eyes, and took a deep gulp of evening air. Then his eyes popped open . . . right on me! He didn't even blink. It was like he *expected* to see me there.

"Hey there, fella," he said. "Don't you have a home to go to?"

I cocked my head and went all gooey-eyed. The smell of him was sweet to me: fresh and scrubbed. His eyes were mild and gentle. All the same, I hung back. It's never good to come on too eager. But then he went down on his haunches and thrust his hand toward me. What choice did I have? I trotted up and gave his fingers a friendly lick. Man, he tasted good!

I had eaten butter once when the dairy wagon tipped over. It was what sunshine would taste like if you could lap it up. That's how this soldier boy tasted.

"You're a friendly little guy, aren't you?" He knelt down and started to scratch me along my spine. *Ahhhhh* . . . This was even better than behind my ear! Nobody had ever scratched my back before. Up to then, I'd had to do it myself by rolling on the ground. This felt *so* much better. It made my lips stretch into a wide grin.

I was practically slobbering with bliss.

"You like that, boy, don't you? You know what I think? I think you're a stray," he said.

I sniffed. I preferred *street dog,* but he could call me any old name he wanted to so long as he kept scratching me.

"I can tell nobody is feeding you. You're built like an armored tank, but your ribs are showing."

Nothing a couple bowls of dog food wouldn't fix, I thought with a sigh as I leaned into his hand.

Suddenly, the scratching stopped! He gave me one last pat, then rose to his feet.

Say! What was the big idea? We were just getting started.

He stretched. "Guess I better get back to my buddies."

I watched with Sad Eyes as he went back inside. Before he shut the door, he turned and shot me a look almost as sad-eyed as mine. I wagged my stub. One wave, and he was gone.

Answering the call of nature, I went around the block to lift my leg on the striped pole outside the barbershop. I wound up having a few heated words through the window with the watchdog chained up inside. The next thing I knew, I came back to find that the restaurant's lights were out and my soldier boy had flown the coop.

But I was sure he'd be back.

At least, I hoped so.

I set up camp by the alley door. I left my post once a day to scrounge around for grub. But I never stayed away for long. When my young man came back, I was going to be there. I was going to lick his buttery fingers. I was going to get my ears rubbed and have my back scratched.

Where've you been? Stinky asked when I saw her at the Dumpster behind the deli. I could tell she was torn. On the one paw, she was happy to see me. On the other, she'd gotten ahold of a half-eaten pork chop. Stinky wasn't big on sharing. Whenever I came too close, she growled. Either the pork or Stinky—or both—smelled a bit off, so I was happy to keep my distance. Besides, I had the soggy end of somebody's salami sandwich, so I was fixed for eats.

I found him, I said.

Found who? she asked between mouthfuls of pork.

My master, I said. *The nice young man of my dreams.*

Oh, brother! Listen to you! Stinky said. *You're an even bigger sucker than I thought.*

Give me another shot at him, and we'll see who the sucker is, I said as I finished my sandwich and trotted back to my post.

Two days later, my soldier boy returned to the eatery. This time, when he stepped into the alley for a breather, he had a present for me. A piece of sweet sausage, right off the griddle!

I scarfed up the sausage and licked the grease

off his fingers. For dessert, he gave me a good, hard back-scratching.

"I wish I could take you home with me," he said.

I smiled. I liked the sound of that!

"But I'm miles from home. *And* in the army. 102nd Infantry Regiment, Twenty-sixth Yankee Division. The Brass says we'll be shipping out anytime. And even if we don't, I'm pretty sure the army doesn't allow dogs in the barracks."

I caught his drift. No Dogs Allowed was a rule I knew all too well. Restaurants, bars, hotels, stores—there wasn't a place in town where dogs were allowed, unless they came in on a leash with their masters, and sometimes not even then.

But, hey, was I going to let a little thing like a rule stop me?

What do *you* think?

Conroy's Dog

It didn't take me long to figure out the habits of my soldier boy. He came to town on the noisiest night of the week—the one you folks call Saturday. Sometimes he went to the same eatery. Other times, I had to go out and hunt him up, him and his buddies. In those days, New Haven wasn't such a big town that I couldn't track them down. I'd pick up their scent and follow it until I found them walking around, singing or poking their noses in shops. Sometimes they'd toss a football in the park, rolling around and wrestling like puppies playing tug-of-war. Wherever my soldier boy was on a Saturday night, I would find him. And once I had him, I would stick to him like glue.

His buddies thought it was a hoot. When they saw me headed down the street, they'd nudge my soldier boy and say, "Hey, Conroy. Here comes your dog."

That was the name of my soldier: Conroy. And to them, that was who I was: Conroy's Dog.

"I wish he *were* my dog," Conroy said one night. "He's a good boy."

"Are you kidding? He's ugly as spit," one of his buddies said.

"Hey, he's not ugly. This dog's got character," said Conroy.

I wondered what character was. Bug eyes and

sagging jowls and a body like an armored tank? If so, then I guess I had character in spades.

One Saturday, after they played football in the park, I followed Conroy and his buddies to where their truck was parked. I watched as they climbed into the back. It was too high for me to jump, and no one offered to give me a boost, so I just stood there. Moments later, the truck started up and began to rumble down the road.

If there was anything I hated, it was being left behind.

I barked, *Hey! Wait for me!*

It was then or never. I ran after that truck as fast as my bandy legs would carry me.

Conroy peered out the back and made a shooing motion with his hands. "No! Stop! Go back, boy! You'll get hurt!" he shouted at me.

But I had no intention of getting hurt. I stayed

clear of the whirring wheels. Still, after a while, my legs got tired and I couldn't keep up. I slowed to a stop and stared after the truck with Sad Eyes. I imagined I could see Conroy's sad eyes staring back as the truck disappeared down the road.

But I wasn't really sad. In fact, I was feeling pretty cocky. Because now that I'd gotten a snoot full of that truck's tires, I knew I'd be able to follow their scent to wherever they'd taken Conroy. But first, I needed to rest up and eat some grub. I pointed my snoot toward the deli and made tracks with the last of my strength. There, I bedded down in some old rags and snoozed until the first rays of the sun peeked over the rooftop of the Chinese joint across the alley.

My pals were lying around scratching at fleas when I broke the news.

I'm off to join my master, I said between bites of

last night's chop suey. *This dog is going places.*

Say it ain't so, Stubs! said Stinky.

We're gonna miss your ugly mug, said Scruffy.

You can always come back if things don't pan out, said Stinky. *And are you planning on eating the rest of that chop suey? 'Cause if you aren't . . .*

I nosed the chop suey over to Stinky.

Help yourself, I said.

With any luck, this would be the last meal on the street I'd ever have. I shook out my coat and got to my feet. *It's been nice knowing you,* I said.

So long, Stubs, old buddy, old pal! they called after me.

I set out after the scent of the truck tires. They were hard to miss. They smelled like rubber and nice young men. Dodging the wheels of automobiles, buses, trucks, and carts, I followed their trail uphill and down dale, past houses, buildings, and more trees than I could lift a leg on. Finally, I came to a big set of metal gates. They were shut tight, and a guard marched back and forth in front of them.

He saw me and stopped. “Get lost, mutt. No dogs allowed on this army base.”

Army base! That meant I had come to the right place. And now that I was there, I was not leaving. My nose told me that Conroy was somewhere beyond those gates. If I could get through them, I could find him. I didn’t want the guard to think I was just some flea-bitten moocher. I wanted him to get the idea that I had an owner on the base. (Which, as far as I was concerned, I did.) So I sat down on my haunches and put a Faithful Dog look on my face.

The guard wasn’t buying it. “You’re looking for trouble, sticking around here.”

I stood my ground. Sooner or later, Conroy was bound to come through those gates. And when he did, I'd give him the biggest, warmest greeting a fellow ever got.

The guard just shook his head. Then things got busy, and he pretty much forgot about me. Trucks and people came and went. The gates would open with a loud clang, and my hopes would rise. There'd be no sign of Conroy, and my hopes would fizzle. The gates would close with another loud clang. *Clang. Clang. Clang. Clang.* That's how it went for the rest of the day. At night, the guard left and a new one took his place.

"What's the story with the dog?" the new guard asked.

"Beats me," said the old guard. "I turned around, and there he was."

When the sun went down, the cold set in. There

was much less activity at the gates now. I found a spot and dug a shallow hole, where I curled up with my head in my tail, such as it was. I dreamt of chasing army trucks down endless roads. Where was my soldier boy? Was I ever going to find him? Had I come all this way for nothing?

In the morning, the new guard left and another came along—eating a fried-egg sandwich. My gut rumbled. I hadn't had anything to eat since the chop suey. I made Sad Eyes at the sandwich and licked my chops. It worked like a charm. The guard ripped off a piece and tossed it to me. I licked my chops again and waited for more.

"You shouldn't be here, dog," he said. All the same, we shared the rest of the sandwich.

Later that afternoon, I picked up a couple of familiar scents. They belonged to Conroy's buddies, who were out for a walk.

I barked loud enough to make myself heard.

"Hey, look," the first one said, "it's Conroy's Dog!"

"I don't believe it," said the second.

They ran over to me.

"Well, I'll be! What's Conroy's Dog doing out here?"

"Looking for Conroy, what do you think he's doing?"

The guard said, "If you know who belongs to this mutt, tell him to please come get him."

"Sure thing," said the guys as they ran back to the camp.

And what do you know? A little while later, who should come walking toward the gate but my dear soldier boy—Conroy! He was a sight for my sore bug eyes. I got up on my hind legs and did a happy little bandy-legged bull terrier jig.

Conroy came through the gate and sank to his knees, laughing. "How did you find your way out here, boy?" he asked.

I fell all over him, licking his chin and buttery fingers.

He laughed and wiped his face on his sleeve. "You followed me, didn't you? You really are one smart pooch."

Then he said to the guard, "I'm pretty sure this dog ran away from his home in town. I'm going to bring him with me into camp. I'll call his owners and have them come get him, okay?"

"Okay, but make it snappy."

Conroy picked me up and squeezed me under his coat. "I'm sticking my neck out for you, boy," he said. "So keep still, and don't make a sound."

This was fine by me. It was very nice under his coat.

Suddenly, Conroy stopped walking. I peered out. We had come to a row of long wooden buildings.

"These are the barracks. This is where I live," he said. He took me behind one of the buildings. "You stay here and be good. I'll bring you some food. Then I'm going to have to figure out what to do with you."

I stayed put. I was, like I said, a good dog. And sure enough, he came back with food and water. He served it to me in two tin bowls.

"Stay here, boy. I'll be back in the morning," said Conroy.

As darkness fell, I dug a shallow hole beneath a bush and got ready to curl up for the night. I was just drifting off, when I heard a horn blow. I jumped up and looked around. As the horn kept blowing, it struck me as the sweetest, saddest sound I had ever heard. I lifted my head and howled along with it. Inside the barracks, I heard the soldiers chuckling.

"That's Conroy's Dog," someone said.

"He's singing 'Taps,'" another one said.

After that, all was quiet except for the peeping of the crickets.

The next morning, another horn roused me from a sound sleep. This one was much perkier than last night's. I leapt to my feet and shook myself out.

Horns to go to sleep to. Horns to wake up to. These soldier boys were some horn-happy people!

I peered around the side of the barracks and saw a line of soldiers with towels around their necks, heading into a shack. They came out a few minutes later with their faces rubbed raw and their hair damp.

After a while, Conroy returned and brought me food.

"I'm off to combat drills," he said. "You're going to have to stay put here."

Whatever combat drills were, I could do them. I sat up and looked lively.

"No. You can't come," he said. "Drills are noisy. You'd hurt your ears something fierce."

Conroy showed up in the afternoon with more food. Then he left again.

Man, oh, man, I was bored! I had definitely not

signed up for this. Was this what being a pet was all about? Sitting around, waiting for your master to return? Maybe my street friends were right. Maybe I wasn't cut out for sucker duty.

That afternoon, while Conroy was off drilling, I cased the joint, making sure no one saw me. Except for a few soldiers sitting around peeling potatoes, the camp was quiet and empty. Were all the others with Conroy? In the distance, I heard explosions, like a whole fleet of trucks backfiring at once. Was this the noise Conroy talked about that would hurt my ears? It didn't sound all *that* loud to me.

When Conroy came with dinner that night, I had to work hard to show some enthusiasm.

"Don't worry, boy," he said before he left. "Hang in there. I've got a plan."

Conroy came back after nightfall carrying a

blanket. He bundled me up in it. "You're coming with me. I don't feel right leaving you out here."

He stood up with me cradled in his arms.

Awww, say, this is swell!

Inside the barracks were long lines of bunk beds and more soldier boys than I had ever seen. Some sat polishing their boots. Other guys lay on

the bunks. As we moved down the aisle, the young men all looked up at me.

"Whoa!" one of them said. "That's the ugliest baby I've ever seen."

"That's no baby," said another man. "That's Conroy's Dog!"

"Conroy's Dog! Conroy's Dog!" they started to chant.

Awww, gee. They were happy to see me!

But Conroy didn't like it. "Pipe down, or Sarge will know something's up," he said. "He'll blow a gasket if he sees I've got a dog in here."

Conroy set me down, blanket and all, on the floor beneath his bunk. "This is where you're going to sleep," he said, "until I can figure out something better."

Little old me? In my own dog bed? Conroy, you shouldn't have!

"Try to be quiet. Remember, you're not supposed to be here," he said.

I squirmed with delight and gave his face a good-night lick. Then I burrowed deep into the blanket.

Just as it did the night before, the sad horn blew.

With an effort, I kept myself from opening my yap and howling.

And it was a good thing I did, because all around me, everyone got real quiet. They stopped what they were doing and climbed into their bunks. The next thing I knew, the lights went out. I was just settling in for forty winks, when the lights flashed back on.

I peered out from beneath the bunk. The biggest, scariest man I had ever seen had just burst through the door.

I'M IN THE ARMY NOW!

The Big Man looked around the barracks slowly, fists on hips. His eyes stopped when they got to Conroy. Then he came striding down the aisle and stopped in front of our bunk. My heart nearly thumped out of my chest. That was one BIG pair of spit-polished boots. I stuck my neck out just far enough to see the rest of him. My bug eyes bugged out, big-time. Everything about him was big: big legs, big arms, big hands, and a big, big red face.

He opened that big mouth of his and bellowed, "Atten-*TION!*"

Conroy leapt from his bunk and stood upright. He bent one arm and hit the side of his head with his hand.

Don't hit yourself, Conroy, I thought. *We'll get through this somehow.*

The Big Man put his face right up to Conroy's. He spoke through bared teeth, like a mad dog. "What's this I hear about a DOG in the barracks?" he growled.

"S-S-Sergeant, sir," Conroy stuttered. "It's true. There's a dog underneath my bunk. I found him in town. He followed me here. He's a stray."

"Is that so?" the man said. He bent down low, and pretty soon I was eyeball to eyeball with the Big Man.

I wanted to scoot out of there with my tail be-

tween my legs. But I was so scared I couldn't move.

He screwed up his face. "What kind of a dog is this, Conroy?" he asked.

"Sir, I'm not sure, sir," Conroy said, still standing tall. "Bull terrier? He's not much to look at, sir, but he's no trouble and he's as smart as a whip."

The Big Man straightened back up. "At ease, Private."

Conroy sagged. The Big Man stared down at me, boot tapping, eyebrow raised.

"So," he said to me, "you want to join the army, do you?"

I crawled out from underneath the bunk.

A feeble growl was all I could manage to squeeze past my lips.

"What's your dog's name, Conroy?" the Big Man asked, not taking his eyes off me.

Conroy muttered, "Er, um . . ."

"Speak up, Private! Dog's got to have a name." He narrowed his eyes, like he really *hated* it when a dog didn't have a name.

"The fellows call him Conroy's Dog," said Conroy with a shy smile.

"THAT'S NO GOOD!" bellowed the Big Man. "A dog needs his *own* name."

I looked up at Conroy eagerly. I knew I had to help him out of the fix he was in. I wagged my stub of a tail and hoped he'd catch on.

He stared at me, looking lost. Then suddenly, his eyes lit up. He raised a finger. "Stubby, sir!

See that little stub of a tail on him? I'm thinking his name is Stubby."

"That's more like it," the Big Man said. He looked down at me. "Stubby, little fella, welcome to the army. Call me Sarge."

I was dreaming about carrying a juicy T-bone steak down Main Street while all my pals looked on, licking their chops. *Eat your hearts out, gals,* I said as I settled down for a good, long gnaw.

Next thing I knew, that perky horn was blaring and my T-bone had disappeared into dreamland. Around me, I heard bed springs creaking and young men groaning. I crawled out from under Conroy's bunk and shook myself hard.

Sarge appeared at the door, fists on hips, red face burning. "Up and at 'em!" he bellowed.

Some of the soldiers were already on their feet.

I scampered at Conroy's heels as he padded out the door.

"Listen, Stubby. It's seven-thirty, and that tune you just heard the bugler playing was 'Reveille,'" Conroy said. "It's French for *time to wake up and get moving.* When the bugle blows at ten o'clock, it's 'Taps.' *Taps* means *lights out, and hit the sack.* In the army, we all do everything together at the same time every day. Right now, it's time to wash up. Uncle Sam wants us clean as a whistle. That's what the latrine is for."

In the latrine there was a long row of shining sinks. The soldiers splashed water on their faces and cleaned their teeth with little brushes. Some of the men lathered up their cheeks with soap and ran a flat metal stick over them. Others stood underneath the spray of a shower and scrubbed themselves, singing at the top of their lungs.

I sure hoped Conroy wasn't expecting *me* to get clean. One time, a street sweeper accidentally splashed me with water. It took me forever to get dirty again. Until I did, I had no idea who I was. A dog's smell is who a dog *is.*

Conroy was busy lathering up his face. "You're lucky you don't have to shave every morning."

Didn't I know it!

When all this cleaning business was over, we headed to a sweet-smelling shack Conroy called the mess hall. He grabbed a tin plate and stood on the chow line. I sniffed it out as we went. We passed a big pot of scrambled eggs, another filled with white mushy stuff, and a griddle loaded up with fried spuds. Maybe it was because I was born in a nest of spud sacks, but I've always been fond of potatoes. I'd eat them any old way, but I especially liked them when they were fried up in bacon grease, which these fine crispy babies were.

The soldiers didn't seem happy about the food.

"I've had *garbage* that tastes better than this swill," the guy in front of Conroy said.

Obviously, this guy had never enjoyed the privilege of eating *real* garbage.

"Belly robber!" another groused to the man who was serving it up.

"Don't look at me," said the man. "I just sling it. I don't cook it."

The men grumbled and made faces. But they choked down the food anyway. Conroy sat on a bench at a long table, elbow to elbow with other soldiers. I squeezed beneath the table, between his feet. Every bite of food came to me served up on Conroy's buttery fingers. I don't know what kind of garbage these soldiers had been eating, but the stuff tasted swell to me.

Afterward, I went with Conroy to a field. It was surrounded by rows of wooden seats.

"This is called the Yale Bowl, Stubby," Conroy said. "Before the war, they played football here. Now we use it to train for combat."

Conroy and the other soldiers carried rifles. I'd seen rifles before, propped on soldiers' shoulders as they marched down Main Street on parade. But these rifles had sharp knives stuck on the ends of them.

"This is a bayonet," Conroy told me. "Dangerous to little doggies."

I gave all the bayonets plenty of space.

I sat on the sidelines and watched as the men marched across the field in long, straight lines.

Sarge caught sight of me and glared. "What are you looking at, soldier? Look lively, and fall in!"

Confused, I stared back at Sarge. Conroy called,

"Here, boy! Stay with me, okay?"

I scrambled until I caught up with him. Then I ran alongside him as he marched. When Conroy halted, I halted. When Conroy turned, I turned. When Conroy lifted his rifle, I stood back and watched out for the pointy tip of the bayonet.

Sarge walked up and down the lines. As he passed, each man raised an arm, bent at the elbow, and hit the side of his head. *Would somebody tell me why these soldiers keep hitting themselves in the head?* You wouldn't catch a dog doing that.

Then the men stood in two long lines, facing each other. Their feet were wide apart, and they aimed their bayonets at the throats of the men standing across from them. I growled at the one with the bayonet pointing at my soldier boy.

"It's okay, Stubby. It's just a game," Conroy told me.

I stopped growling, but I didn't like this game.

Sarge strolled along, correcting the way the soldiers held their rifles. He said, "The bayonet can be a good friend to only *one* man—you or your enemy. Your life depends upon your learning how to handle it. Your hold should be firm, but relaxed. Your stance should be balanced and solid. You don't want your opponent to push you off your feet. Then your goose is cooked."

Sarge went along and tried to push the soldiers over. Some of them stumbled and fell. Conroy got a good, hard shove, but his feet stayed planted. *Conroy's goose is safe,* I thought.

After bayonet practice, the men marched in line with their rifles over their shoulders.

"About FACE!" Sarge barked.

The men all turned to face Sarge.

"Present ARMS!" he shouted.

The men held their rifles out in front of them. Sarge walked along and looked at the guns. Then he stood back and barked some more. The men lowered the rifle butts to the ground. Then they lifted them from the ground to their shoulders. Next, they picked the rifles up and went down on one knee. They peered down the barrels of the rifles.

"Prepare to fire!" Sarge yelled.

The men put their fingers on the triggers.

"FIRE!"

STOWAWAY!

I was sure I was a goner. The sound knocked me clean off my feet. I squeezed my eyes shut and never expected to see daylight again. All around me, rifles EXPLODED. It was the loudest sound I had ever heard, louder than the Town Center Park on the Fourth of July when they set off those pesky fireworks.

When the noise died down, I blinked and opened my eyes.

I was still in one piece. The air was thick with smoke. My ears were ringing like the bell on the knife sharpener's cart. My fur—what little I had—was standing on end. And I was shaking like a whippet on a block of ice.

Conroy touched me, and I nearly jumped out of my skin.

"Easy, boy," he said. He patted me, smoothing my fur and speaking in a soft, gentle voice. Finally, I managed to calm down and regain my bull terrier cool.

"These are combat drills, Stubby. We're practicing to fight in a war," he explained. "The bullets are blanks, so no one will get hurt, but they still make plenty of noise. We've got to get used to the racket so we don't lose our heads in battle. If you want to be in the army, you'll have to put up with it."

I wasn't sure about the army, but I sure wanted to be with Conroy. And after a few days of drills, I did get used to it. In fact, it got so that when the soldiers fired their rifles, I just panted and grinned. Bring it on, boys!

One afternoon, the guys lined up and charged at a row of soldiers. They shouted and stabbed at the men with their bayonets—and straw flew out of their bodies! *What is this craziness?* I ran around and barked my fool head off. Then Conroy showed me that the soldiers were just uniforms stuffed with straw. That was a relief! Still, I had to admit I liked rifle practice better than this squirrely business with the bayonets. Something about all that stabbing and yelling and flying straw just set me off.

One day after lunch, when we were back in the Yale Bowl, Conroy knelt before me on the sidelines and took my head in his hands. I stared at him. Today, he was wearing a helmet.

"Stay," he said.

I watched as Conroy and the others got down on their bellies. Hugging their rifles and slithering along on their elbows like big snakes, they made their way through the grass. Slowly but surely, they were all crawling away from me.

Have I said that I really hated being left behind? Sad to say, I hated it so much that I disobeyed Conroy. I got down on my belly and crawled until I had caught up with him. It was a little hard on the elbows, but kind of fun. Next thing I knew, something came whistling through the air and exploded nearby. The earth beneath me shook. The soldiers covered their heads with their arms as bits and pieces of rock and earth rained down on us. I covered my head, too, for all the good it did. This

was no fun after all. I guess I should have stayed put like Conroy had told me.

But Conroy wasn't mad. He was proud. "That's my brave boy, Stubby," he whispered to me from beneath his arm.

Easy for him to say. He had that nice hard helmet on his head.

Helmet or not, I hadn't lost my head. But it ached a bit from all the noise and excitement. I was glad to see that no one had gotten hurt, although a lot of the men had a spooked look about them. Maybe they were thinking the same thing I'd been thinking: *If this was just practice, what would the real thing be like?*

And so it went, day after day: "Reveille," latrine, mess hall, and drills, drills, drills. By the time the bugle boy blew "Taps" each night, I'd be curled up in my doggie bed, all tuckered out. It didn't take me long to learn the routines and exercises so well that I could do them in my sleep. In fact, I woke myself up one night, covering my head with my paws as a shell exploded in my dream.

One evening, after chow and just before "Taps," Conroy said to me, "I've got something for you, boy."

More food? I thought. Call me an optimist.

It was almost better than food. It was a dog collar. A nice sturdy leather one, not like those frilly collars I'd seen on some pets in town. This one was army-built and just right for me. Conroy put it around my neck and buckled it. It made a nice jingling sound when I moved.

"Sorry it doesn't have a tag on it. That's 'cause you're here unofficially," Conroy said. "And now for a new trick."

Conroy had already taught me some tricks. I knew Sit and Stay and Heel and Roll Over and Play Dead. I was ready to learn another.

He took some pieces of dried beef out of his pocket. I sat up tall. So far, so good.

"Present ARMS!" he said to me, just like Sarge said to him. He picked up my paw and touched it to the side of my head, just above my eye.

What exactly did this noodle-head have in mind? Did he expect me to hit myself in the face like the rest of them? If he did, he had another think coming.

He gave me a piece of beef. I ate it.

He stood back. “Present ARMS!” he said. He stared hard at me.

Huh? I stared hard back at him. He couldn’t possibly want what I thought he wanted.

The other young men in the barracks gathered around to watch.

“Give up. You can’t teach a dog to salute, Conroy,” one of them jeered.

“He doesn’t even *have* arms,” said another.

“You just wait. He’s a smart dog,” Conroy said. Once again, he demonstrated, bending his arm and hitting the side of his head.

“Let’s try again,” he said. “Present ARMS!”

If you can’t lick ’em, join ’em, I always say. This time, I lifted my paw and tapped the side of my head. It was a little sloppy, but it was the best I could do with what I had.

The young men burst into cheers. They were so busy tackling Conroy, pounding him on the back, and messing up his hair that he forgot he owed me. I tapped him on the knee.

"Oh, right," he said, tossing me a bit of dried beef. "You earned it."

As it turned out, this particular trick would eventually save me from a watery grave.

One day after morning mess hall, the soldiers in the barracks stuffed all their gear into long canvas bags. Then they heaved the bags over their shoulders and headed for the door. I looked around as, one after another, they disappeared. What was up? I didn't like the looks of this.

Conroy was the last to go. That was when I

started to worry. I made Sad Eyes at him.

"We're shipping out today, Stubby, but don't you worry. I'm not leaving you behind. I just have to hide you from the transport officers."

Conroy held open his barracks bag. He'd crammed everything down deep inside of it so that there was just enough room in the top for me. I crawled in and turned around to face the opening. Conroy pulled the drawstring, leaving just enough of a hole for me to breathe through. I could peer out with one bug eye. Then—*ooof*—he heaved the bag over his shoulder and marched us out of the barracks.

We passed Sarge on our way to the truck.

"Glad you could make it, Private Conroy," he said, rocking slowly on his heels. "And as far as I'm concerned, there is no dog in your barracks bag. Others in command might not be quite so willing to turn such a blind eye. So watch yourself."

"No, sir. Yes, sir," said Conroy.

"Good luck over there, soldier," Sarge said. "Take care of yourself, and watch out for the furry little guy."

"Yes, sir."

The truck ride was dark and bumpy and smelled like gasoline. "The furry little guy" was feeling sick to his furry stomach. I told my growling guts to settle down and quit beefing. It could have been worse. At least Conroy hadn't left me behind with Sarge.

When we got to the train station, Conroy let me out long enough to lift my leg on the tracks. Then I got back into the bag. "We have to stow our gear in the baggage car, Stubby. You're going to be alone for a while. Keep your head and lie low, okay?"

I licked him to let him know that I'd be a good dog. Wasn't I always?

Conroy saw to it that my bag was on the top of the pile so I wasn't squished. He loosened the top so I could come and go to do my business. I kept my head and lay low. But it was lonely in the baggage car. I fell asleep to the *clickety-clack* sound of the train on the rails. Every now and then, I would scooch out of the bag and lift a leg in the corner. Then I scooched back in. There were cracks in the side of the baggage car, and the wind whistled through, making a low, lonesome sound. What with one thing or another, I was a miserable wreck.

Finally, someone shouted, "Newport News, Virginia—last stop!"

The train stopped with a long, loud chuff of steam. I smelled salty sea air and saw seagoing birds like we sometimes got in New Haven wheeling in the sky.

Conroy came for me. When he peered into the bag, I was shaking all over. He looked worried. He opened his coat. "Climb in here. I'll keep you warm."

Gratefully, I crawled out of the bag and under his coat. He buttoned me in tight. I peered out between the buttonholes, and what did I see? This great, big, hulking thing bigger than a whole block of buildings floating in the water.

"That's our ship," said Conroy. "It's going to be our home for the next few weeks."

I wasn't a big dog, but I was no teacup poodle, either. With me under his coat, Conroy waddled up the gangplank. Luckily, the ship's officers were too busy to notice the bulge beneath Private Conroy's coat. Either that, or they figured he was one fat soldier boy.

Conroy was waddling along a corridor when his friend caught up with him. I stuck my nose out to say howdy-do. The buddy didn't think I was one bit cute. He grabbed Conroy by the sleeve and whispered in a harsh voice, "Are you *nuts* bringing him to your cabin? I hear this captain runs a tight ship. The last pet that stowed away got tossed overboard."

I didn't know where overboard was, but it didn't sound good. I sure hoped Conroy knew what he was doing.

Conroy halted and stroked his chin. "I never thought of that," he said.

After some dithering, he started climbing down a whole bunch of ladders. Down and down we went, until we were at the very bottom of the ship, where the engine was. It hummed so loud, Conroy had to shout to make himself heard. He stashed me away in a nasty little room where they stored the coal to feed the engine.

"WHEN THE ENGINE GUYS COME IN TO SHOVEL UP THE COAL—HIDE!" Conroy said. "AND WHATEVER YOU DO, DON'T LET ANYBODY SHOVEL YOU INTO THE FURNACE."

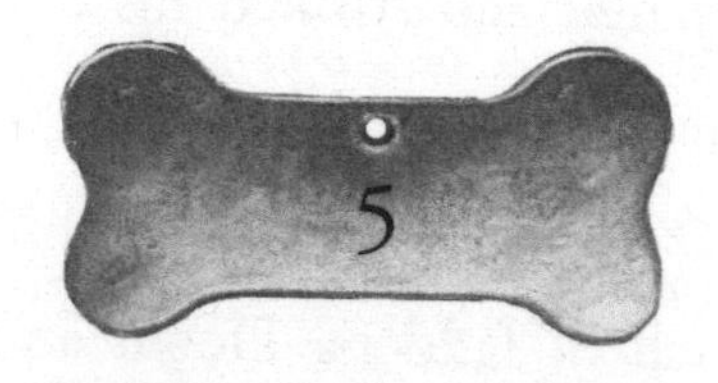

Advice from a Horse

Conroy came down twice a day to feed and water me and pick up my business. I kept hoping he would take me up for a walk in the fresh air. After all, I was a street dog, and I liked my freedom. Down there, I felt like a prisoner. The loud, steady drone of the engine was beginning to get to me. I was ready to bust out and make a run for it, when Conroy came to my rescue.

"YOU NEED SOME AIR!" he shouted over

the engine's roar. "I'M GOING TO TAKE YOU UP ON DECK FOR A FEW MINUTES."

If you think it's easy for someone to climb a half dozen ladders while holding a quivering dog, you're wrong. How Conroy managed to do it I don't know. But eventually he did, and we were up on deck.

Fresh air! Birds! Sunshine! Ocean waves!

I leapt out of Conroy's arms. I was free!

Some soldiers were standing around. "Stubby!" they cried when they saw me. They were all grinning, ear to ear.

Before I could say hello, I had to shake myself out. Black coal dust, like a storm cloud, billowed off of me. The soldiers stood back and laughed.

"Conroy, you're a genius!" one of them said.

"Stubby's a stowaway!" another said.

"Hurray for Stubby!" they all cried.

I ran back and forth, jumping up and licking everyone. I was so pleased to be out of the coal room and back with my boys that I got up on my hind legs and did my happy little bandy-legged jig.

The men circled round and stomped their feet and cheered. "Stub-by! Stub-by! Stub-by!"

Suddenly, the cheering stopped.

A tall, thin man marched over and broke through the circle of soldiers. Everybody pulled back. Only Conroy stuck by my side. But he looked plenty scared. The tall man was dressed differently from the soldiers—all in white. Something told me he was the man in charge. This was the seagoing Brass.

I stopped dancing, dropped to all fours, and hung my head. From the look on the man's face, I was in for it.

"What's THIS, Private?" the man roared at

Conroy. I tried to hide behind Conroy's leg.

"It's a dog, sir," Conroy said in a small voice.

"I'm aware of that, Conroy. But how did THIS DOG get on board my ship?"

Conroy gulped. "I smuggled him aboard, Captain, sir."

I looked up at Conroy and whimpered.

"I don't know how you do things in the army, Private, but in the navy, we don't allow dogs. The last dog that snuck aboard this ship got fed to the sharks."

The captain pushed his hat back and wagged his head, like he was sorry for what was about to happen but there wasn't much he could do about it, was there?

My heart skittered in my chest. I was sorry, too. I looked to Conroy. Couldn't he do something?

Conroy said, "Don't just stand there, Stubby.

You're in the presence of the captain of the SS *Minnesota.* Atten-TION!"

Pulling myself together, I sat down and looked lively.

"Present ARMS."

I lifted my front leg and snapped that captain the smoothest military salute ever made by a dog, on land or sea.

Before he knew what he was doing, the captain answered with a salute of his own. Then he caught

himself and began to laugh. "Well, I'll be hornswoggled!" he said. "If it isn't a little soldier dog!"

The men fell all over each other, joining in the mirth. I didn't see what was so funny. That salute was close to perfect. And it had saved my neck.

The captain shouted, "Machine mate—front and center!"

A mate ran up and saluted. "Yes, sir!"

"Go below and make this soldier a dog tag."

I know what you're thinking. When you hear the words *dog tag,* you think of those metal tags people put on their dogs with their address on them. But this here was another kind of dog tag. It was the kind the U.S. Army issues to soldiers. Stamped into the metal are their name, rank, outfit, date of birth, and the proud letters *USA.*

Conroy was grinning like crazy later that day when he attached my dog tag to my collar.

If only my buddies back in New Haven could see me now!

After a few more weeks at sea, the ship finally docked in a place called Saint-Nazaire in the faraway land of France. Now we had a whole new set of commanding officers to hide me from. To get me off the ship, Conroy tried something different. He dressed me in his coat with my head sticking out of the collar like I was a soldier. I was nowhere near as tall, so he and his buddy had to hold me up. They walked me down the gangplank like they were supporting a guy who was unsteady on his feet. There was so much happening on the dock that nobody seemed to notice that one of the soldiers had a furry face and was floating about three feet off the ground.

It was exciting to be in a new place. New

smells, new people. We even had a new name—the American Expeditionary Forces. We were the first full outfit to land in France. They trucked us to a camp where we'd be holed up for a while. The Brass wanted us to train some more and get used to being in France before they sent us up to the Front.

What was the Front? The Front marked the spot where the two sides—our guys and the enemy—were fighting to win territory. I was no stranger to this idea. It was just like dogs on the street haggling over turf. The meanest, strongest, baddest dog won. I wondered, *In this war, who would that be?* All I knew was that I was there to help, in any way I could, like the good dog that I was.

Our first camp in France was like a town made out of tents. Conroy and I slept in a tent with five other guys. There was a mess tent and a latrine tent and a communications tent and a first aid tent and even a tent where they showed moving pictures. I didn't get out much, as you can imagine, being a dog in hiding. I spent most of my time under Conroy's cot. He smuggled me scraps from the mess, mostly salmon and beef.

As careful as Conroy was, it didn't take the new commanding officer long to get wind of me.

"You mean to tell me this dog came all the way from Yale Field?"

"It's kind of a long story, sir," Conroy said. Once again, he launched into it. How we met in town. How I followed him to Yale and latched on to the 102nd. How I drilled and trained and prepared to fight to give my life for my country, just like the rest of the boys. When he was finished, even I had a lump in my throat. What a touching tale!

By the time Conroy ordered me to salute, the

commanding officer was one hundred percent sold on me staying with the regiment. What was he going to do, anyway? Send me to Paris to hang out with French poodles? Besides, he said I was good for morale, whatever morale was. He made me the mascot for the 102nd Infantry, Twenty-sixth Yankee Division. It was official. From then on, the only people I had to hide from were the enemy.

In our new camp, the soldiers learned all kinds of things. They got lessons every day from a bunch of French soldiers. Our boys learned to build barracks in the field. They learned how to read French maps. They practiced how to operate machine guns. These are big guns that make an *ack-ack* sound that's hard on a dog's ears. They also learned to toss grenades without blowing themselves to bits. Grenades are metal things that look like small footballs. I watched one day as Conroy pulled the ring out of the top of one, counted to five, and then tossed it. A moment later, there was a gigantic explosion. Some football! But the men spent most of their days learning about trench warfare.

What was trench warfare? It doesn't exist today. But that was mainly how war was fought in Conroy's and my time. A trench is a long, narrow hole in the ground. First the men poked around to find good, dry dirt to dig in, so their trench wouldn't fill up with water. Now a dog would never have to *learn* how to dig a proper hole. We are born knowing how, with paws that are built for digging. We dig holes to sleep in, to bury stuff in, and sometimes just for the sheer joy of digging. But for men? It's work. And it's a skill they have to learn.

In the gear the soldiers carried strapped to

their backs was something called an entrenching tool. This is a fancy name for a shovel. Not being blessed with paws, the men needed shovels to dig the trenches. These trenches were deeper and wider than any dog had ever dug—as deep and wide as a man is tall, sometimes even wider. And the trenches didn't run in straight lines. They zigzagged all over the place so the enemy wouldn't know where they were.

After the trenches were dug, the men lined the top edges of them with sandbags. These were supposed to stop bullets from going into the trenches. Good idea, right? Then the soldiers set up camp in the trenches and made themselves at home. Imagine! Men living in burrows like packs of wild animals. That's war for you. They slept there, ate there, yammered there, did their business there, and read letters from home there. Every day, they practiced crawling up to the top of the trenches behind the sandbags. They rested their guns on the bags and fired them. Sometimes the bugler sounded a call and they went charging over the tops of the trenches, hooting and hollering and firing away. Between hooting and hollering, rifles blasting, grenades bursting, and machine guns *ack-acking,* there was a regular racket going on. It's a good thing I'd gotten used to the noise back in New Haven. Otherwise, I'd have headed for the hills on day one!

Mornings and nights, the soldiers chowed down on rations. Rations were what they called the food that was stored in tins and boxes that the government handed out. It wasn't always the freshest stuff, but it kept us going, and I, for one, couldn't get enough of it.

Like all the soldiers, Conroy carried a haversack. In it, there was a plate, a cup, a knife, a fork, a spoon, and the all-important (if you ask me) meat can. There was almost always something good in the meat can. Naturally, Conroy shared it with me. Afterward, he poured water from his canteen into his cup, and I lapped it up. Living in a trench made you thirsty. At night, the soldiers sat around and talked in soft voices, even though the enemy was far away. They were practicing being quiet. *Shhhh.*

"When are they going to send us to the Front?" one of Conroy's buddies complained.

"Quit your bellyaching," another soldier told him. "We'll be risking our necks soon enough."

From what I had come to understand, this war had been going on for a good three years, since before I was even born. So far, it had just been the English and the French fighting against the Germans and a bunch of other guys. And it looked like the Germans and their friends were winning. That was because they had more men and bigger guns—like the one they called Big Bertha. We Americans were Johnny-come-latelies, pitching in now to help the English and the French.

The French soldiers teaching the Americans were hardened by their time fighting. I could tell they didn't think much of our boys. In fact, these Old Sweats—as experienced soldiers were called—thought the American Expeditionary Forces were a bunch of green lads. *Green* means inexperienced and ignorant. Much as I hated to admit it, they might have had a point. The Americans looked like fresh-faced kids. Next to them, the Old Sweats looked ancient. I felt sorry for all of them—the Old Sweats because of what they'd been through, and my boys for what they were about to go up against.

Nights, I got a little restless, and I would climb

out of the trench and go exploring. In my wanderings one time, I ran into a surprising number of horses. They stood around with their feed bags tied on, munching away.

Sidling up to one of them, I asked, *What's a nice horse like you doing in a place like this?*

The horse stopped munching and gave me a look. Then he went back to his oats.

He was a tough old boy, not all that friendly, the kind who did his job and minded his own business. Still, I wanted an answer so I kept at it. *So, buddy, tell me, how did you get here?*

The horse probably figured I wasn't going away until my curiosity was satisfied. He said, *If you must know, I was drafted by the quartermaster's office. I was a farm horse in Iowa. I pulled a plow and minded my own business. Then one day a man came along and took me away from my family. He shipped*

me overseas, and I've been here ever since, serving good old Uncle Sam. There are thousands of us who were taken from our paddocks and stables and brought over here.

Now I got it! When I was a small pup, the streets

of New Haven were full of horses pulling carts and wagons. Then one day, it seemed like they all disappeared. I'd wondered where they'd gone to, and now I knew. They were here!

Have you been to the Front? I asked. I was dying to hear more about it.

Plenty. At the start of the war, the soldiers rode us up there in cavalry charges. But we never stood a chance against those big German guns. They mowed us right down, man and horse. Now we go up there to haul supplies to the men in the trenches: rations and ammunition and artillery, medical and building supplies, and tons of mail. The cavalry days are over. It's all about trench warfare these days.

Tell me about it, I said. *I've worn my nails down to the pads digging trenches.*

You'll be digging more before your hitch is up, said the horse.

I don't mind. I've lived in worse places, I said.

Wait until you get to the Front. When the enemy starts bombarding, you won't think those trenches are quite so cozy. I'll be getting back to my feed now. You watch out for yourself. The battlefield is dangerous. It's no place for a little dog.

Don't worry about me, I said. *I was a street dog. I can take care of myself.*

Sure you can, tough guy, said the horse, going back to his munching.

I could tell he didn't believe me. One thing was for sure: this horse had given me some things to think about. Like, *what have I gotten myself into?*

As I turned to go back to the trenches, the horse called out to me, *And for pity's sake, whatever you do, watch out for the gas!*

Gas? What was gas? And why in the world did I have to watch out for it?

DOUGHDOG

After five months of itching to see some action, word finally came down—we were moving to the Front. And just like that, all the cheerful chatter stopped. The men fell silent as they packed their gear. This was it. Real war, not just practice. We were going to a place called Chemin des Dames (shih-MAN day dom). That's French for *road of the ladies.* As we made our way there in the bitter cold, we saw the damage that war had left in its wake.

Everything that was once living and green had been scorched to cinders, leaving a sea of mud. The soldiers slogged through it up to their hips. For a dog with stubby legs, it was nearly impossible. Conroy heaved me over his shoulder and carried me. Now and then, we'd hit dry stretches. He would set me down and let me walk.

Whenever we passed field hospitals, the wounded soldiers would rear up on their cots and call out to us.

"Good luck!"

"God help you!"

"Leave the dog with us. We'll take care of him!"

"Don't worry. So will I!" Conroy told them as we marched on.

We made our way past bombed-out buildings, wrecked wagons, dead horses, and whole forests of blackened trees. And of course, more mud.

"I know it looks bad," Conroy told me, heaving me back up onto his shoulder. "But we're in this together."

It's you and me, doughboy, I growled, and licked the flour off his chin.

Doughboy. That's what they called the American soldiers. No one was sure why. Maybe because the men were given flour to bake their own biscuits? My boys weren't exactly bakers. The flour got all over them, and me, too. I had to wonder, did that make me a doughdog? Sometimes they called us Americans Sammies, as in Uncle Sam.

We, on the other hand, called the British soldiers Tommy, the French soldiers Frogs, and the German enemy Jerry. Why? I hadn't a clue. Maybe it cheered the men up to call people names. But I didn't care for it. Even when I lived on the street, where things got pretty rough, I never went in much for name-calling. When it came to cheering people up, I did my bit, fair and square. I wagged my stub of a tail and tried to keep a wide grin on my chops at all times. So far, that was my biggest contribution to the war effort.

When we got to Chemin des Dames, the soldiers took out their entrenching tools and started digging. After the men were settled in, I ran all along the trenches, making sure everybody was safe. The soldiers saw me and grinned, their teeth bright in their muddy faces. By then, everybody in the unit knew me. When they called my name, I stopped to say hi and to give them a chance to scratch my back. By the time I returned to Conroy, I saw that he had dug a hole in the side of the trench. Good man! It was called a dugout. This was where we would bed down.

Things were trench-normal for the first few

days. That's army-talk for Quiet with Nothing Much Going On. Then one day, out of the blue, the enemy attacked. Machine guns *ack-acked.* Bullets whizzed overhead. Mortar shells exploded. The sky turned dark and oily with smoke. Between the shells exploding and the artillery pounding, it was enough to make my head burst. This was definitely not what I'd had in mind the day I followed that army truck out of town. But I was determined to make the best of it.

"Stay down, Stubby, or you'll get your head shot off," Conroy warned me. He didn't have to tell me. Seeing as how I was fond of my head, I lay low when the bullets flew.

Conroy and the other soldiers lay on their bellies behind the sandbags and shot back at the enemy. The bags jumped when bullets hit them. Bullets pinged off the soldiers' metal helmets.

The excitement got to be too much, and I started to bark. Not at my guys, of course. At the enemy. It might seem like a pretty lame exercise for a dog to bark in the face of gunfire, but I couldn't just hide. I had to do *something.* And barking's one thing we dogs know how to do.

The men didn't mind me doing this. But they minded plenty when I did my business in the trench. So during lulls in the fighting, I would go out to lift a leg. There were two sets of coiled barbed wire, one that ran along our trenches, and the other about half a city block away in front of the enemy's trenches. Barbed wire is razor sharp. I learned this the hard way when I rubbed up against some one time and got a bad scratch. Conroy had to put medicine on it that stung like the dickens, so now I didn't tangle with the stuff. The area between the two rows of barbed wire was called No Man's Land. There were strips of No Man's Lands all across France.

On the day I'm talking about, I lit out for No Man's Land to do my business. I found a nice big gap in the barbed wire to squeeze through. There was nothing out there but shell craters and tree stumps and charred bushes. I caught sight of one of our soldiers lying on the ground. He was moaning.

I rushed to his side.

"Hey, Stubby," he said weakly. "What are you doing out here? It's dangerous."

I might have said the same for him. He must have left the trench to get a better shot at the enemy. But they had gotten him first. I offered him what comfort I could. His face was bleeding, and I licked it. The blood tasted saltier than rations. There was more blood on his uniform where he clutched a hand to his side. Suddenly, I saw a couple of medics with a stretcher. I barked as hard as I could to let them know where we were, and stayed with the wounded man until they carried him off. After that, I went on a search. On that day alone, I found nine more soldiers. Sad to say, three of them were dead. I kept the medics on their toes.

When the shooting started up again, I hightailed it back to the trenches. All around me, bullets cut into the earth. Who would shoot at a dog?

I liked to think it was nothing personal. Maybe I was just in the way. Then again, maybe they didn't like little mutts. *Grrrr.*

Conroy fell down on his knees when he saw me. I tell you, that man hugged me so hard it hurt. "Stubby, you scared me half to death. Where have you been? You can't wander off like that. This is war!"

I hated upsetting Conroy. But I knew I would wander off again. Because now there was a way I could really make a difference in this war. I could help wounded soldiers stranded in No Man's Land.

One day, during another lull, I sneaked out to lift my leg on a blackened bush. I was going about my business, when something came flying through the air and landed, *ka-thunk,* at my feet. It was a strange-looking metal canister. I gave it a wary sniff. Before I could figure out what was inside,

the thing cracked open and began to hiss like an angry cat.

My eyes started to burn. My knees buckled. My head spun, and I staggered around. Then I keeled over into the mud.

I dreamt I was back in the alley. Apron Man came out of the eatery. He picked up a handful of gravel and threw it at me. The gravel was red-hot. It burned my face and chest.

When I woke up, I couldn't see a thing. My

nose wasn't working too well, either. But my ears were fine. I could hear Conroy, and I could feel his hand resting gently on my chest. I tried to let him know that I was okay. But for the life of me, I couldn't move a hair on my body. I might as well have been a dog made of stone.

"Hey, Doc Burns. I felt a twitch," Conroy said. "I think he just woke up."

"He's lucky to be alive," said Dr. Burns. "He was right on top of that gas canister when it went off. When I think of people gassing an innocent dog . . . That's what I call a war crime."

Gas canister? My mind drifted back to the moment when the strange hissing object landed by my foot. Then I remembered what the army horse had said: *Watch out for the gas!*

The next time a horse gave me advice, I was going to listen.

Ever heard the expression *sick as a dog*? Well, I was sicker. My stomach burned like I'd swallowed hot coals, and my eyes were glued shut. My lungs itched so bad I could have stuck my paw down my throat and scratched . . . which I would have done if I could have moved a muscle . . . which I could not.

To his credit, Conroy stayed by my side. The constant murmuring of his voice was my lifeline.

"You've got to get better, Stubby. I can't make it through this war without my best buddy. The whole outfit is rooting for you to pull through."

I heard him, sure, but I was trapped inside the stone dog. I just lay there, like a lump.

"You were gassed, Stubby," Conroy said. "The doc's been giving you oxygen and rinsing your eyes with water. But I'll be honest with you, little guy, the doctors aren't positive you're going to make it.

That mustard gas is bad stuff. It's not the kind of mustard you put on a hot dog. It's poison. The worst weapon ever made. They call it the King of Battle Gases. We all have gas masks to wear—the guys are making one for you. You're going to wear it, too, in the next attack."

I groaned inwardly. The next attack? There was going to be another?

I don't know how long I lay there. Maybe days. Conroy began to get desperate. I could hear it in his voice. "Just give me a sign, Stubby—one little sign that you're getting better. I'm trying not to lose hope here, but it's getting hard."

Maybe it was the pleading edge I heard in his voice. Maybe I was just ready to snap out of it. But suddenly, I felt my tail start to twitch.

"Stubby!" Conroy shouted. "Atta boy!"

The next thing I knew, my bones were creaking

and I was sitting up. I opened my gluey eyes one at a time. I saw tears rolling down Conroy's cheeks. He was grinning like a fool. How I'd missed the sorry sight of that soldier boy!

"You did it! You pulled through! You're gonna live!"

I gave out a little woof. Of course I was alive. I wasn't ready to push up daisies yet. With a bone-dry tongue, I gave his buttery fingers a lick. The taste made my mouth start to water. I kissed Conroy, and darned if he didn't kiss me right back, all over my sorry mug.

A Four-Legged Warning System

When I got discharged from the hospital, it was back to the good old Front. Everybody was thrilled to see me. I took a run up and down the trenches, checking in with everyone to make sure they'd been okay while I was out of commission. By the time the shooting started up again, I was stationed on top of an ammunition case, barking and howling fit to burst. How dare they fire at my boys! How dare they?

I was in such a lather that Conroy stopped shooting long enough to have himself a good chuckle. "You've worked yourself into a regular battle rage!"

I was angry, all right.

Early one morning, I was cozied up in the dug-out next to Conroy. I'd gotten myself wedged in his armpit, where I could feel his breath ruffling the top of my head as he snored away. The enemy had come down hard on us the night before. Now that the fighting had let up, everybody was fast asleep. I had been, too. But all of a sudden, I was wide-awake.

My nose twitched. The hair along my spine stood straight up. *There is something wrong.* Deep in my gut, where the last drop of the mustard gas still burned, it was starting to bubble and boil and talk to me.

It was saying, *I'm gonna get you this time, mutt.*

I aimed to listen.

I licked Conroy's face. *Wake up. Something's coming. Something bad.*

Conroy groaned and shoved me away. "Lay off. Go back to bed."

I went into his gear and dug out his gas mask. I dragged it over to him. *Here, put this thing on. The gas is headed this way.*

Don't ask me how I knew. Maybe being gassed had made me sensitive to the smell. Or maybe I was just being a nervous Nellie. But no matter how convinced I was, Conroy didn't care. All he wanted to do was sleep.

I started running up and down the trench, sounding the alarm. The men groaned. I nipped at them, tugging at their coat sleeves and pant legs. Just like Conroy, they lay there like dummies.

Don't you get it? You're in danger. I lifted my head and started to howl.

One of them clapped his hands over his ears. "Put a sock in it, Stubby!"

"Conroy!" another soldier moaned. "Tell your dog to shut his fuzzy yap!"

But I was *not* going to shut my fuzzy yap. Not until they wised up, woke up, and listened up.

Finally, one of Conroy's buddies shook the sleep out of his head. He gave me a look. "What's the matter, Stubby? What's got you so riled?"

I got up on my hind legs and danced. But this was no happy little bandy-legged bull terrier jig. This was the Dance of Danger! Then—finally—it dawned on him.

"Hey, guys," he said slowly, "I think the dog is trying to tell us something."

"Like what?" asked another guy. "He's hungry?"

"No. Like maybe there's a gas attack headed this way."

At the mention of *gas,* the other guy was suddenly kicking free of his sleeping bag. He clawed his way over the sandbags and peered around. I crawled up beside him.

It looked like dawn mist, all innocent, blowing from the direction of No Man's Land.

But we both knew better.

That mist was gas, wafting toward us on the morning breeze.

"GAS!" the soldier hollered. "Gas attack!"

The men started to wake up. And it was about time they did! I headed to the other trenches, zigzagging my way along, barking the alarm.

Everybody was on their feet now, fumbling for their gas masks. I ran back and checked to see that Conroy had put his on. He looked like a

monster when he wore it. But it didn't scare me. What scared me was gas. I climbed into the dugout and burrowed into his sleeping bag until there was nothing showing but my tail.

After that, silence. All I heard was the rasping of the men breathing through their masks.

Maybe Mother Nature had given me some kind of gas meter in my tail, but somehow I sensed when it was safe to come out. I backed out of the bag, shook myself all over, and took in a big lungful of air. I could barely detect a trace of the stuff.

One by one, the men took off their masks. They crowed with relief and crowded around. Conroy hugged me so hard my bug eyes bugged. He gave my back a good, long scratching until I was just one big, slobbering grin.

"No two ways about it. You saved us, Stubby," he said.

Aw, shucks. It was nothing.

"The next time you kick up a fuss, we'll listen."

Afterward, Conroy gave me most of his morning rations. Some of the other men tossed me scraps from theirs. My belly was full, and my boys were safe. All told, I was feeling pretty good about the way things had turned out.

I never did get around to wearing the gas mask the fellows made for me. It wasn't that I didn't appreciate their thoughtfulness. It was just that I'd sooner dive into a sleeping bag than let somebody strap that doohickey on my head. Sometimes after I issued my warning, I didn't even stick around. I'd hotfoot it off until the deadly cloud blew over. Either way, the stuff never got me again. And I like to think that the King of Battle Gases claimed far fewer soldiers with Stubby the four-legged gas alarm keeping watch.

It was April in the lovely land of France. But you'd never have known it to look around. Everything that had once been alive and thriving—trees, flowers, bushes, grass, birds, bugs, bunnies, squirrels—was dead or had wised up and vamoosed.

We were on the move again, trudging through the wasteland to a place called Seicheprey (SESH-eh-pray). It was a tiny town, surrounded by what was once farmland. On one side, for as far as the eye could see, lay the woods they called Foret de Mort Homme (for-AY de more um). That's French for *dead man's forest.* (Cheery, eh?) Apparently, this area was supposed to be the *quiet* part of the Front. We dug our trenches, and all was quiet . . . for a spell.

The mail came. Nothing cheered the boys up more than mail from home. Letters from sweethearts and sisters arrived, smelling sweet as flowers. Letters from mothers came, smelling like the cakes and pies they packed for their boys. The baked stuff got a little dinged up from handling, but it tasted fine. There were other presents, too: sausages, cheeses, and lumpy, hand-knit sweaters and socks. After mail call, I made it a point to do the rounds. The boys never denied me my share of the goodies.

Then early one fine, spring morning, the enemy hit us with everything they had. They were like a big dog showing us—a little dog—we had no business on their turf. On the second day of fighting, they sent in units armed with weapons like hoses, shooting fire instead of water. The enemy moved fast, hit hard, and burned everything in their path. Then they ran back across No Man's Land to their trenches. Our guys were fighting mad! When the bugler sounded the call, our guys swarmed over the tops of the trenches and went hard after the enemy. I was right there with them.

As soon as they saw us coming, the enemy unloosed their artillery. My ears twitched at the soft clicking sound that told me a shell was on its way. I hit the ground and buried my nose in my paws. When Conroy saw me, he shouted to the soldiers, "Artillery shell! Hit the dirt!"

Just like me, the men dived for the ground and shielded their heads. Moments later, the shell burst. The earth erupted and resettled itself. I looked up and shook the dirt out of my eyes. Then I ran around to see if anyone was hurt. But the men had picked themselves up and started running again. From that point on, the men kept one eye on the enemy and the other on me. When I dived for cover, they did likewise.

When the enemy saw us charging across No Man's Land past the barbed wire, they swarmed out of their trenches to meet us. For the first time, my soldiers were fighting hand to hand. Everybody fought in this battle, including the cook (with his meat cleaver) and me (with my teeth).

I saw an enemy soldier sneaking up on one of my boys and gave out a sharp bark of warning. The American whipped around in time to defend

himself. Next, I came upon a German and an American soldier with locked bayonets. The German pushed the American off balance. I snarled and grabbed the German's bootlaces and tugged, giving the American time to regain his footing. I clung to that boot like a burr. Finally, the soldier was so irritated that he turned on me. But I was too fast. I ran away before he could stab me with his bayonet.

I was staring into the thick of the battle—firing rifles, flashing bayonets, flying fists—trying to figure out where I could lend a paw, when a grenade landed right by my leg. Before I could run clear of it—*kaboom*—it exploded.

The blast knocked me squeegee, blowing me backward.

The next thing I knew, Conroy had picked me up like a football and was running back behind our lines. I was bleeding all over. He took out his field dressing and wrapped my leg and chest in bandages. He gave me a few gentle pats, then ran back to help our boys.

My leg and chest throbbed with pain while the battle raged on. The bandage was soon soaked with blood, and I tore at it with my teeth. I needed to get to the wounds and lick them. But I was too weak to do the job. I lay back in the dirt, exhausted. As I swirled off into a deep darkness, I wondered whether this was curtains for me.

A Decorated Dog

By the time Conroy came back, the sounds of the fighting had died down. He lifted me in gentle arms and ran through the wreckage until we got to the field hospital.

Conroy charged into the tent. "Wounded dog here!"

He laid me on a cot. Soon a familiar face loomed above. Well, what do you know? It was my old pal Dr. Burns.

"Stubby!" said Dr. Burns. "Not you again!"

I tried to work up some enthusiasm, but even wagging my stub took more strength than I had in me. I was hurting bad.

"He followed us over the top and right into battle," Conroy said to the doc. "You should have seen him. The little man was in there fighting just like the rest of us."

"Is that true, Stubby?" the doc said with a wide grin. "Are you a fighter? From the looks of you, I'd like to see the other guy."

Conroy held me down while the doc took a pinching tool and removed the shrapnel buried in my leg and chest. Shrapnel are sharp little bits of metal from the exploded grenade. Each time he removed a piece, I let out a yelp.

Ouch! Ouch! Ouch! That Dr. Burns sure earned his name that day!

He tossed the pieces into a can, where they made a *ping-ping-pinging* sound.

Conroy made calming noises.

"This is gonna hurt me more than it hurts you," Dr. Burns said.

Yeah, right.

When the doc was finished, he put some stinging medicine on my wounds and wrapped me up in fresh bandages tighter than a package sent from home.

Afterward, I fell into a deep sleep and woke up with my teeth chattering. I was cold all over. Conroy was still with me.

"I think he's got a fever," he said. "His nose is warm. Is he going to be all right, Doc?"

"I don't know. I'm not a vet, and I'm not really equipped to treat a dog here. We'd better get him to the Red Cross Recovery Hospital," the doc said.

Uh-oh. The Red Cross was where they sent the soldiers who were hurt bad. They had more doctors and more medicine.

"I'm going, too," Conroy said. "The commanding officer told me I should stick with him."

After that, I passed out. The next time I woke up, I was lying on a cot in a strange new place. Conroy was sitting beside me.

"Hey, boy. You're coming along okay."

Slowly, I tried to make sense of where I was. Man, but I was stiff and sore! Around me, there were cots, every last one of them filled with a wounded soldier. All of them looked pretty banged up. Suddenly, I didn't feel so sick. Before Conroy could stop me, I jumped off the bunk and went to work.

I trotted up and down the aisles, stopping at each cot. *Hey, howya doing, soldier?*

Some of the guys were so bandaged up, you could hardly see their faces. But most managed to reach out a hand to pat me. Others were too weak to do much of anything, their skin sweaty and their breathing short. I gave these guys a good, strong swipe of my tongue. I licked whatever part of them I could reach and told them to hop to and start getting better. *I did it,* I said. *I came back from a gas attack and an exploded grenade. You can get better, too.*

They kept me at the Red Cross until they were sure my wounds were healed. Every day I was there, I made my rounds. Then I would take position near the entrance, where the medics brought in the wounded. When these boys came in, scared and hurting, guess who was there to offer a friendly face and a warm lick.

Everything's going to be all right, I told them. *You're safe now. The folks here know what they're doing. Take it from me.*

When I was being discharged, the doctor said to Conroy, "That dog of yours is the best medicine these men could have. Come back and visit sometime—but not on a stretcher, okay, Stubby?"

Hey, he didn't have to tell me twice.

I got back to the Front just as the battle was winding down. With the worst over, I went into No

Man's Land and helped the medics track down the wounded. By then, I knew all the ambulance drivers and medics, and they knew me.

All in all, in spite of casualties, this had been a successful campaign. We were able to drive out the enemy and recapture the village of Seicheprey.

I dared anybody then to call my boys green. The boys of the 102nd Infantry, Yankee Division, were seasoned soldiers and brave men, every last one of them.

By the end of June, we were on the move again, traveling by train to the next battlefield. The men were ragged and dirty. But with a solid victory behind them, they were feeling cocky. We got out at a station northwest of a place called Chateau-Thierry (SHA-toe teary), where we joined up with the French forces and prepared for battle. Again, the men dug trenches. Conroy's hands had become hard and calloused from digging. Once we were hunkered down, the American and French soldiers put their heads together and plotted. They whispered to avoid being overheard. The enemy was clever, covering their uniforms with branches to make themselves look like bushes. Then they snuck behind enemy lines and listened in.

While the men were talking, I rested. I was a little out of shape and needed all my strength.

Our plan was to launch a surprise attack on the enemy while they slept. The night before the battle, we all hit the sack early.

"I've got butterflies in my stomach," Conroy said to me. "You watch yourself tomorrow, boy."

We were up before dawn. Quietly, we ate our rations in the dark. The soldiers checked their gear and weapons. Then, at 4:45, we climbed out of the trenches and started moving toward enemy lines.

In their hobnailed trench shoes, their long coats flapping, they ran silently across the scarred and pitted ground of No Man's Land, toward enemy territory. I ran with them.

As we came upon their trenches, we saw that, except for a few drowsy guards at the end of their watch, the soldiers were wrapped in their sleeping bags, dead to the world. Somebody on our side blew a whistle, the shrill noise piercing the dawn. The men raised their rifles and began to fire into the trenches, shouting as they bore down.

And that was just the beginning of many hard days of battle alongside the French soldiers. Moving in advance of us, the French tried to take a German-occupied hill and failed. We stalled out behind them. Finally, we pushed through and liberated the town from enemy occupation.

In the days that followed, in dribs and drabs,

the good people of Chateau-Thierry returned to find that the city was theirs once again. They were grateful to the American Expeditionary Forces. One night, torches burned, and soldiers and villagers sat around tables in the square. They pooled together what little food they had to make a feast. The ladies patted me and made goo-goo eyes. Conroy explained to them with his few French words that I was no ordinary pet.

I was *un chien extraordinaire,* he told the ladies. He told me that meant *extraordinary dog*. He told them that I was a brave soldier who had been wounded twice. He boasted about how I warned the men about gas attacks and artillery barrages. It was enough to make even a bull terrier blush.

Conroy must have impressed the ladies, because later on, in another town, they held a special ceremony where they presented me with my own

army jacket. It was made of soft leather and fit like a second skin. On it they had sewn badges showing all the battles I had fought in. When they wrapped the jacket around my shoulders, they kissed the top of my head. I sat proudly and raised my paw to give them my smartest salute.

Now, thanks to the lovely ladies of Chateau-Thierry, I was a decorated soldier.

Bagging a Spy

We stopped for a few days so the men could get fresh uniforms, new gear, and a chance to rest. Then we pushed northward by train to the region of St. Mihiel (san me-HEL). There, we marched through what seemed like endless woods, clearing out enemy troops as we went. One day, Conroy gave me the good news.

"It looks like our side is winning now, boy."

So it was a little surprising that, there in the

woods of the Argonne, we wound up running into our hardest fighting yet. It seemed like the enemy had saved their best soldiers to defend this very important site, close to the capital city of Paris. Every day, our boys struggled to move forward and push the enemy back. Many soldiers died fighting. That—and the *ack-ack* of the machine guns and the *zzzzzz* of the fighter planes overhead—was bad enough to make even a seasoned soldier dog turn tail and run. But as long as Conroy and the rest of the regiment forged ahead, then so would I.

When we were too exhausted to march another day, we stopped and dug trenches, hoping for a day or two of rest. As usual, I wandered out into the countryside to do my business. I was looking for a bush that hadn't been blown to smithereens, when I came upon what I knew right away was not a bush. It was a soldier disguised to *look* like a bush.

He had leafy branches sticking every which way out of his belt and collar and boots. Just who did he think he was fooling? Any fool could smell that he was a man, not a shrub. (Although it would have served him right if I had lifted my leg on him. Ha!) His head was down, and he was scribbling on a pad, the kind the boys used to write letters home.

I bared my teeth and growled.

He stopped and looked up. When he saw me, he smiled and held out his hand. "Good doggie," he said. "Come here."

He spoke the language of the doughboys and Tommies, but he wasn't fooling me. He was no doughboy. He was a Jerry! A German soldier! I lifted up my head and started barking. *Look who I've caught, boys, a stone's throw from our trenches!*

The smile died on his lips, and his eyes widened in terror. "Hush! Hush! Good doggie!" he whispered. "We would not want to cause a stir."

Oh, yeah? A stir is *exactly* what I aimed to cause.

When he saw I was not going to quit, he turned and made a run for it. I took off after him, hurling myself onto his back and toppling him over head-first into the dirt. His pad and pen went flying. He struggled to push himself up. But I sunk my teeth into what I know to be tenderest part of a person's body.

You guessed it: his rear end!

I heard running feet approaching.

Five American soldiers appeared. Four held guns trained on the German. The fifth picked up the man's writing pad. He looked at it and chuckled.

"Well, what do you know!" he said. "This guy's been mapping the locations of our trenches. Looks like Stubby caught himself a spy."

"At ease, Stubby," another soldier said. I

opened my mouth and released the enemy's butt. He groaned and rolled over, then stumbled to his feet, hands raised behind his head.

"I surrender," he said. "Get this vicious dog away from me, please."

Vicious? Hardly. Just doing my duty like any red-blooded American soldier would do. And speaking of duty, I trotted off in search of a *real* bush to lift my leg against. In war, as in peace, a dog's gotta do what a dog's gotta do.

* * *

According to the Brass, the enemy was ready to surrender. Well, the day couldn't come too soon for me. We marched on from the Argonne to another resting place called Mandres en Cotes (mond on coat). It was November, and the men got Thanksgiving turkey in their meat cans. At the camp, we did drills and exercises, and the Brass held ceremonies where they gave speeches and moved soldiers up in rank or pinned medals on heroes. At one ceremony, Conroy got promoted from private to corporal. But the real kicker was that I got promoted.

Conroy looked down at me and grinned. "You outrank me now, Stubby. Or should I say, *Sergeant* Stubby?"

Didn't that beat all?

A month later, at Christmastime, at a place called Humes, there was a big commotion in HQ. (That stands for headquarters, where the Brass hangs out.) The men were told to wear their newest, spiffiest uniforms. I wore my jacket with all its badges and medals. Conroy put on his new jacket with the corporal stripes. That morning, we practiced drill marches on the parade field, just like we did back at Yale. A strange man was standing with the Brass in the review stand. He was the only one not wearing a soldier's uniform.

As we came to attention before the stand, the soldiers seemed extra alert and a little bit nervous. I looked up at Conroy, wondering who this new guy was. But Conroy was way ahead of me.

"Don't look now," Conroy said out of the corner of his mouth, "but that man up there is the president of the United States, Woodrow Wilson. He's come all the way over here for peace talks. It's a pretty big deal."

I must not have looked very impressed, because he added, "He's not only the leader of our country, but he's the commander in chief of all the armed forces."

Well, why didn't he say so in the first place? I was looking at the biggest Brass there was!

"The war you helped fight is almost over, Stubby," Conroy said.

After the review, he took me to meet the president.

"So you're Sergeant Stubby," the president said. "I've heard a lot about you."

Like most everyone, my jacket impressed him. He noted all the medals on it. There were the ones the ladies of Chateau-Thierry had given me. And other ones I'd gotten since then, including the German cross from the spy I nabbed.

"You're a brave soldier, and your country owes

you its deepest gratitude," he said to me.

"Don't just stand there, soldier," Conroy said to me. "Present ARMS!"

I lifted my paw and gave the leader of the United States Armed Forces one snappy salute.

Instead of saluting back, he held out his hand. I lifted my paw, and we shook. And suddenly there I was, Stubby the New Haven street mutt, shaking hands with the president of the United States. Who'd have thunk it?

At Ease

One day I woke up, and something wasn't right. It was Conroy. He was shaking like a Chihuahua in a meat locker. I crawled up to his head and gave his face a lick. He tasted salty and sweaty. And his skin was so hot it scalded my tongue!

Conroy? Conroy? Talk to me, buddy!

"I'm not feeling too well, Stubby!" Conroy said through chattering teeth.

Uh-oh. Now I was worried. Gas, bullets, *ack-*

ack guns, spies. There was lots to be scared of in this war, but one of the scariest things was called the Spanish flu. It was a bad, bad sickness. We lost lots of soldiers to the Spanish flu. But I wasn't about to lose Conroy. I lifted my head and started howling.

Pretty soon folks came running, wanting to know what the fuss was all about. Then they got a look at Conroy's pale, sweaty face and they knew.

"Call the medics," one of Conroy's buddies said. "He's got the flu!"

Somebody gave Conroy a dribble of water from his canteen, but Conroy just spat it up. Where were those medics? What was taking them so long?

Finally, two of them showed up carrying a stretcher.

Over here! I barked. *On the double!*

As they loaded Conroy up, I couldn't keep still.

It was all I could do not to nip at the medics' heels. They were moving too slowly! Conroy's face was too pale!

I chased after the stretcher as the medics ran with it to the field hospital.

There, the nurses crowded around Conroy. I got tangled up in their feet. One of them practically tripped over me. They shooed me away, but I kept coming back. I had to know that Conroy was all right. We'd been through so much together. I couldn't lose him now!

One of the doctors came to look at Conroy. He was new, and we hadn't been formally introduced. When he saw me, he frowned. "No dogs allowed!"

A nurse said, "That's Stubby, doctor. Conroy's dog. He's just making sure we do a good job taking care of his master."

She had that right.

The doctor said to the nurse in a low voice, "The war's over for this soldier."

Well, THAT got my attention, I can tell you that.

The doctor said, "I'm going to ship him off to the American Hospital in Paris. As soon as I get authorization and a free ambulance, that's where he's headed. Of course, the dog will have to stay here."

I lifted my head. My lips started to curl. A deep growl vibrated in my gut. I was a whisker away from taking a bite out of this guy. How *dare* they separate Conroy and me! Not even the Germans had succeeded in doing that, and they had tried awfully hard.

"With all due respect, doctor," the nurse said, "Stubby is probably as important to Corporal Conroy's recovery as medicine. You're new to the Front, sir, but I've been here for months. And I've seen the wonders this dog has done for the sick and wounded."

"Is that so?" the doctor said. "In that case, I'll see what I can do."

While we were waiting for the transfer to come through, Conroy began to get a little better. He and I slept like we hadn't slept in months, like a couple of babies. Every so often, I'd wake up and leave him alone just long enough to make the rounds and visit the other wounded soldiers. I was allowed to go where I needed to go and to lick whoever needed attention. Now and then the doctor stopped and gave me a good scratch on the back. I guess that meant we were on friendly terms now.

The ambulance finally came. When they loaded Conroy up, the doctors, nurses, medics, and patients who were strong enough to stand all lined up outside the field hospital. They saluted me. I returned their salute, and then jumped in the back of the ambulance next to Conroy.

The doctor stuck his head in. "I've put on your chart that Stubby needs to stay with you no matter what. If anyone gives you any guff, tell them to get in touch with me."

The ambulance ride was rough going over the bumpy roads to Paris. Conroy was strapped onto his stretcher, but I was banging around loose like a marble in a jar. By the time we got to Paris, I might have been more in need of a doctor than Conroy!

We stayed in the Paris hospital until Conroy cooled down and could stand up without getting dizzy. I walked with him through the streets of Paris. The sight of an American soldier made the locals so happy! The women hugged and kissed him on both cheeks, the men shook his hand, and the soldiers saluted us both. My saluting amused the Parisians.

After a couple of weeks in Paris, Conroy got his ticket home. He packed up our gear. My soldier boy was returning to the States a hero. You would have thought, after all I had done for the war effort, that I could travel like the rest of the soldiers. But that was not the case. Just like in the bad old days, Conroy had to hide me in his cabin and smuggle me out on deck wrapped up in his coat. The only difference was, Conroy's coat was worn, dirty, and ripped up now—a lot like me, with my scarred chest and legs and my scorched lungs. We had been through four offenses and seventeen battles—and had lived to tell the tale.

We went home, not to the base in New Haven but to Conroy's real home in Massachusetts, where his mom and dad waited for him. I liked Conroy's place just fine. His mom and dad smelled buttery, like him, minus the gunpowder and wet boots. They were so glad to see us! They folded Conroy in their arms and wept with happiness. They hugged me, too. I didn't know whether to salute them or kiss them. So I did both.

"We've heard all about you from John's letters," his teary-eyed mom told me. "Welcome to our home."

I'd never lived in a house before. When I was a street dog, a home was all that I longed for. Since meeting Conroy, I'd lived in barracks, tents, trenches, and hospitals, but never in a house. It was warm and comfortable and quiet. I slept with Conroy in the room that had been his as a boy. When I needed to do my business, he let me outside. But he always welcomed me back into the house.

I was just getting used to the place, when Conroy said we had to leave.

He dressed me in my jacket, and he put on his uniform.

I couldn't believe it! What was the deal? Were we going back to war?

Conroy just laughed. "Don't worry, boy. This is going to be fun."

Together, we boarded a train bound for a place called New York City, where the Hotel Majestic made an exception to its No Dogs Allowed rule. They let me stay with Conroy in his very fancy room. The Brass there even gave me a bone for my dinner and another for my breakfast.

We continued by train to the city of Washington, D.C. There, Black Jack Pershing, one of the tip-top army Brass, presented me with a special award. I sat next to him on a table, and he gave me a medal to wear around my neck on a chain. It was gold and my name was spelled out on it, according to Conroy. I saluted. The crowd clapped.

Other awards followed. The YMCA gave me a lifetime membership and three bones a day for the rest of my life. I marched in parades with the old soldiers who had fought in previous wars. I raised

money for the Red Cross. At American Legion conventions, I met two more American presidents, Harding and Coolidge, both dog-lovers, from the smell of them.

After a while, we made a return trip down to Washington, D.C., where Conroy was going to study at a place called Georgetown University. Once again, there were No Dogs Allowed, but they made an exception for me. In fact, they were so taken with me, I was made the official mascot for the Georgetown football team! On a field a lot like the one in New Haven where I first trained to be a soldier, I learned a new trick—pushing a football with my nose. It was not all that clever. Truth to tell, I sometimes felt just a bit foolish doing it. But it drove the crowds crazy. They cheered and tossed me flowers and treats. They chanted my name.

"Stub-by! Stub-by! Stub-by!"

And once again, I was a hero. What a life!

But the hero business aside, what I really liked best was being with Conroy. He'd sit at his desk reading great big law books, and I'd lie by his feet, dozing and dreaming. Every so often, he'd reach a hand down, and I'd give it a lick for old time's sake.

It's a fact that war is a mean and low-down thing. A world without war would be a much better place. But Conroy and I had learned that some things are worth fighting for. I liked to think that I served Uncle Sam to the best of my ability. But most important of all, I served Conroy. And I continued to serve him until the day I was ready to be planted in Soldiers' Field. Until then, I enjoyed the good life. And in my book, it just doesn't get any better than that.

APPENDIX

Great War, Great Dog

The causes of World War I were numerous and complex. The single event that many say triggered it occurred on June 28, 1914, when a Serbian patriot—who sought independence from the Austro-Hungarian Empire—assassinated the heir to its throne, Archduke Franz Ferdinand. This shocking event prompted the Austrian-Hungarians to declare war against Serbia. Russia and Germany, who were vying against each other to build their own empires, were quick to choose sides. Russia came to the aid of Serbia. Germany allied with Austria-Hungary. When Germany invaded France through Belgium, France joined the war, and Britain soon followed. The Turks sided with Germany. The Italians joined France against Austria-Hungary. Soon it seemed like all of Europe had piled onto the bloody, multinational heap that would later be known as World War I. At the time it was fought, however, most everyone called it the Great War.

What was so *great* about it? The sheer brutality of its weapons, for one: airplanes, U-boats (which we now call submarines), machine guns, and poison gas. Its range, for another: from the Atlantic Ocean in the west across Europe to the Russian Empire in the east and south as far as the Persian Gulf. Its consequences were certainly great, resulting in the destruction of old empires—Austria-Hungary's Hapsburg, Russia's Romanov, and Turkey's Ottoman—and the formation of new countries, such as Czechoslovakia, Syria, and Yugoslavia. And certainly the casualties were great: over

37 million dead, including civilians and military.

American president Woodrow Wilson did everything he could to keep the United States out of the Great War. It was a European turf dispute, he said, and the U.S. had no stake in it. The war raged on for three years while the U.S. remained in isolation. But in April 1917, Wilson had had enough. He went before Congress to get their support for America's entering the war. The reason he cited was that Germany had violated its pledge to suspend submarine warfare in the North Atlantic and the Mediterranean. But it was Germany's secret attempt to lure Mexico—America's neighbor to the south—into the war that might have been the final straw. On April 4, 1917, the U.S. Senate voted to support Wilson's declaration of war. Two days later, on April 6, 1917, the House supported the motion. The United States declared war on Germany.

The 102nd Infantry Regiment, Twenty-sixth Yankee Division, with Stubby in tow, were the first to make up the American Expeditionary Forces. They were shipped to France in June 1917. There, on the battlegrounds of France, the Twenty-sixth fought the longest—210 days—and sustained the greatest number of gas casualties of any American unit. For a bunch of green boys from New England, they fought hard and bravely. In fact, the Germans considered them one of the four best assault divisions in the U.S. Army. Fighting alongside his master, Private John Robert Conroy, Stubby participated in all four major offenses—St. Mihiel, Meuse-Argonne, Aisne-Marne, and Champagne Marne—and in seventeen battles, including Chemin des Dames, Seicheprey, and Chateau-Thierry. He was wounded twice, first by gas and later by grenade. In Donremy, the birthplace of Joan of Arc, the grateful ladies of Chateau-Thierry presented Stubby with his own chamois army jacket, having lovingly sewn onto it medals and decals marking his career campaigns.

Stubby had earned every one of those medals. He warned the men about gas and mortar attacks. He caught a German spy by the seat of his pants. He kept up morale in the trenches. And in every field station and Red Cross hospital he visited, he offered comfort and encouragement to the wounded and sick. By December 1918, when President Wilson came to Humes, France, to review the troops on his way to negotiating a peace settlement, Stubby's exploits had made him as famous as he was beloved.

Stubby returned stateside following the Armistice to a hero's welcome. In a highly publicized ceremony, General "Black Jack" Pershing, Supreme Commander of the American Forces, presented Stubby with a gold medal minted by the Humane Education Society (a forerunner of the Humane Society). Naturally, Stubby saluted the general with his paw, just as Conroy had taught him to do at the start of the war. The YMCA granted Stubby lifelong membership, including three bones a day. He posed for paintings, participated in parades, and raised funds for the Red Cross at American Legion conventions, where he met two more presidents—Harding and Coolidge. When John Conroy went to study law at Georgetown University, Stubby accompanied him to Washington, D.C. There, Stubby became the official mascot of the university football team, the Hoyas. In what might have been the earliest known version of the halftime show, he entertained fans by pushing a football across the field with his nose—a far cry from dodging sniper fire on the battlefields of Europe. But the crowds adored him.

Stubby died in Conroy's arms at the age of ten, but he was not buried in Soldiers' Field. The remains of the most decorated dog in military history were preserved. You can visit them in Washington, at the National Museum of American History, a part of the Smithsonian Institution. In addition to Stubby himself, you can see his collar, his harness, a scrapbook kept by John Conroy, and Stubby's spiffy army jacket, which still sports his numerous war medals and souvenirs. The German cross he got off the spy, unfortunately, seems to have disappeared. While the evidence of that escapade has vanished, the tale lives on. It is only one chapter in the long story of the little bull terrier mix who fought hard alongside his master, lending his great valor and heart to the Great War.

For more information about World War I, check out a site sponsored by the U.S. Department of State:

- history.state.gov/milestones/1914-1920/wwi

The National World War I Museum's website includes activities and educational information for kids and families—plus downloadable lesson plans for educators:

- theworldwar.org/learn/kids-families
- theworldwar.org/learn/educators-students

To read more about Stubby, visit the terrific Smithsonian site at:

- amhistory.si.edu/militaryhistory/collection/object.asp?ID=15

War Dogs

Dogs have been used in wars since ancient times. As early as 327 BC, Alexander the Great conquered the known world with the help of a giant war dog called a molosser, who wore a studded collar. Most likely an ancestor of today's mastiff, the molosser could supposedly hold its own against a lion. In 236 BC, armor-clad dogs fought alongside the Roman legions. Farther north, in 55 BC, the Britons used mastiffs with spiked helmets to ward off the invading armies of Caesar. Much later, in 1798, another conqueror named Napoléon chained dogs to the walls of Alexandria to warn of the approaching British troops.

Dogs worked in the American Civil War as mascots and message carriers. Yet in 1917, when Stubby was smuggled aboard the SS *Minnesota,* there were no dogs serving in the U.S. Army.

Stubby wasn't the only unofficial canine participant in the Great War. Rags was a French stray adopted by the Eighteenth Infantry Division. He carried messages behind enemy lines and, like Stubby, warned of gas attacks. Dogs like Stubby and Rags paved the way for war dogs in years to come.

After the Japanese attack on Pearl Harbor in December 1942, breeder organizations like Dogs for Defense campaigned for the official use of dogs in the military. They encouraged owners to donate their working dogs to the war effort—preferably German shepherds, Doberman pinschers, collies, Belgian sheepdogs, Alaskan malamutes, and huskies. With the help of the American Kennel Club, they raised funds to train and recruit a formidable canine force. But the demand for war dogs was greater than Dogs for Defense could handle. That's when the military pitched in with the War Dogs Program. By 1943, the two groups cooperated to draft over 10,000 dogs. The dogs were trained to serve in various capacities: as sentries, attackers, scouts, pack and message carriers, casualty seekers, and mine sniffers. But unlike Stubby, none of these dogs were desensitized in advance to the noise of gunfire. As a result, many cowered at their first exposure to battle. Fortunately, most of them eventually grew accustomed to the noise. Ever since, desensitization to gunfire is one of the first lessons a canine military recruit learns.

Dogs have played key roles in every modern war, from Korea to Desert Storm to the war in Iraq. War is an unpleasant and regrettable fact of life, but dogs continue to offer their invaluable assistance to the military, loyally and obediently following their soldier handlers into the fray without a moment of hesitation or a woof of complaint.

For information on the history of U.S. war dogs, go to:

- jbmf.us
- uswardogs.org

More About the American Staffordshire Bull Terrier

Stubby was a street dog with no papers—a mutt. But some believe that, based on his looks and behavior, he was probably an American Staffordshire bull terrier mix. In England, the Staffordshire bull terrier came about as a result of breeding the bulldog with the Manchester terrier. Originally bred to bait bulls, the bulldog had strength and tenacity. The terrier had agility and high spirits. The result is an agile, shorthaired, medium-sized dog with great strength for its size and a never-say-die attitude. Farmers in the Staffordshire region of England found it useful as an all-purpose farm dog. The breed first came to America in the 1870s and was accepted in the American Kennel Club in 1936 as the American Staffordshire bull terrier. Ranging from fourteen to sixteen inches and weighing anywhere from twenty-four to thirty-eight pounds, the American "Staffy" is heftier than its British cousin. It is loyal, intelligent, eager to please, has a sense of humor, and loves people, particularly children. It is important to note that the breed tends to be very protective of its loved ones.

For more information about this wonderful breed, go to:

- akc.org/breeds/staffordshire_bull_terrier/index.cfm

Owning an American Staffordshire Bull Terrier

These dogs often get a bad rap. Because of their strength and history as bull baiters, some people use these dogs (and dogs with similar physical traits) for the illegal and abusive practice of dog-fighting. Dogs trained to fight other dogs understandably have trouble mixing in everyday life. But when properly trained and socialized, this breed can make a first-rate pet. Just ask any loving family who owns one. They'll tell you that Staffies—or AmStafs—are, in the noble tradition of Sergeant Stubby, affectionate, intelligent, brave, gentle, funny, loyal, and possessed of an emotional makeup that is uncannily near-human.

For more information on owning or rescuing an American Staffordshire bull terrier, visit:

- amstaff.org

Stubby and Miss Louise Johnson in 1921 in the Humane Education Society parade